Weekly Reader Presents

Cotterpin's Perfect Building

By Ellen Weiss · Pictures by Lauren Attinello

Muppet Press
Henry Holt and Company
NEW YORK

Published by Henry Holt and Company,
521 Fifth Avenue, New York, New York 10175.

Library of Congress Cataloging in Publication Data
Weiss, Ellen.
Cotterpin's perfect building.
Summary: After their assistant architect designs the Perfect Building, the Doozers of Fraggle Rock stop building things and must cope with the resulting boredom.
[1. Buildings—Fiction. 2. Architecture—Fiction.
3. Puppets—Fiction] I. Attinello, Lauren, ill.
II. Title.
PZ7.W4472Co 1986 [E] 85-18923
ISBN: 0-03-007244-1

Printed in the United States of America

ISBN 0-03-007244-1

This book is a presentation of
Weekly Reader Books.

Weekly Reader Books offers book clubs for children
from preschool through high school.

For further information write to:
Weekly Reader Books
4343 Equity Drive
Columbus, Ohio 43228

BRIGHT and early one morning, Cotterpin Doozer grabbed her lunch pail and set out for work.

If you know any Doozers, then you must know what Doozers love to do. They love to build. They make buildings and bridges, towers and spires. Fraggles, of course, like to eat Doozer buildings, which is fine with the Doozers because that makes room for more buildings.

But Cotterpin was a different sort of Doozer. She *hated* building. Instead, she loved drawing. That's why Cotterpin worked as the assistant to the Architect. The Architect designed and drew the plans for all Doozer buildings.

When Cotterpin arrived at the Doozer Design Office, she found the Architect standing on his head in the middle of the floor.

"Ah-ah-CHOO!" he sneezed loudly. "I've got the sneezing fits. It happens every now and then. If I take care of myself and stand on my head, it goes away in four and a half days. Ah-ah-CHOO!"

"Gee, that's terrible," said Cotterpin. "Is there anything I can do to help?"

"Well," said the Architect, "I think I'll just go home. Could you—ah-CHOO!—take over until I come back?"

"Could I? You bet!" said Cotterpin excitedly. Then she remembered that she shouldn't look too happy. "You just get some rest. I'm sure I can handle the job."

Cotterpin sat right down at her drawing table and took out her pencils and rulers. She was so excited she could hardly think straight. She was in charge, really in charge! She could try all the daring designs that were buzzing around in her head. She could finally show everybody what beautiful Doozer buildings she could think up.

In fact, Cotterpin decided to draw the most wonderful thing the Doozers had ever made—or ever *would* make. Cotterpin was going to design the Perfect Building.

First she tried a triple-arched high rise with wrap-around balconies. It was one of her favorite ideas.

The building was nice, but not quite special enough. So she kept drawing. She tried a double-decker dome and a pop-up pyramid. Then she drew a split-level palace with built-in fountains. But none of them was really the Perfect Building.

Cotterpin went to bed late that night. She still didn't have her design, but she needed some sleep. Then, in the middle of the night, her eyes popped open. "I've got it!" she said. "I've finally got the design for the Perfect Building!" She jumped out of bed and began drawing madly. When the sun came up, she was done.

“Wake up, everybody!” she shouted. “We’re going to build the most beautiful Doozer building in the universe!”

Now, Doozers are not like Fraggles. They aren't interested in singing or dancing or whooping it up. They don't tell jokes, and they don't tickle. But if there's anything that gets a Doozer excited, it's the idea of building something really special. So pretty soon every Doozer in Fraggle Rock was as excited as Cotterpin about the Perfect Building.

"Let's build it over in Echo Cavern," suggested Cotter-pin. "It's out of the way, so nobody will bother us before it's finished."

"Good idea," said everyone.

The Doozers began working on the Perfect Building. Cotterpin's drawings were very good, and the work went quickly.

For two entire days, every Doozer was busy. Radishes were made into Doozer Sticks, forklifts buzzed to and fro, beams were hoisted into place, joints were welded, plans were double-checked.

Then finally the last pegs were hammered in. It was finished.

"*Wow!*" gasped Crankshaft.

"Gee *whiz!*" squeaked Socketwrench.

"Dazzling Doozerdom!" said Sandpaper. "It sure is something."

"Well," said Drillbit after the Doozers had admired the building for a while, "I guess we should let the Fraggles eat it."

"Seems sort of a shame," said Crankshaft. "It's really nice."

"Sure is," sighed Cotterpin. She was feeling miserable just thinking about her wonderful building getting eaten.

Then she brightened up. "I have an idea," she said. "Why don't we string up some radish ropes all around it so nobody can touch it? And maybe we could take turns guarding it so the Fraggles can't eat it."

"We've never done that before," said Ratchet.

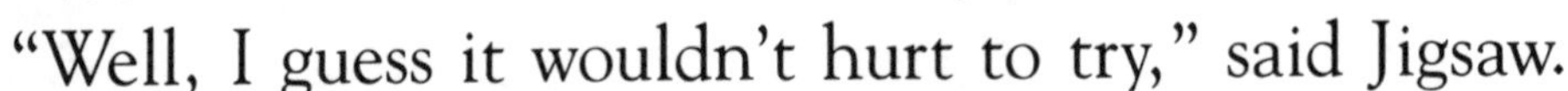

"Well, I guess it wouldn't hurt to try," said Jigsaw.

"What'll we do now?" asked Crankshaft after they had finished roping off the building.

"I don't know," mused Cotterpin. "It's kind of hard to go back to making regular old buildings after finishing one like this, isn't it?"

"Um . . . sort of," said everybody.

"I have another idea," said Cotterpin. "Why don't we try doing something else? We could play games. We could have hobbies."

"We've *certainly* never done *that* before," squealed Socketwrench.

"Well, I guess it wouldn't hurt to try," mumbled Drillbit, "for a little while."

The next day, the Doozers tried playing games and having hobbies. They had radish-rolling races. They played Pick Up Doozer Sticks. They collected nine different kinds of cave moss.

But by midafternoon, it was clear to everyone that this wasn't working. Nobody was having any fun.

From time to time, some of the Doozers wandered into Echo Cavern to have a look at the new building. But something funny was starting to happen.

"It certainly is lovely," said Sandpaper, "but maybe if it was just a bit higher over there, it would be even more lovely."

"Hmmm," pondered Crankshaft. "Isn't it just the teeniest bit squatty?"

By evening the *hmmm*'s, the *but*'s and the *maybe*'s had spread. Everyone agreed that the new building was very fine but that there could be even better ones. And what's more, the Doozers wanted to build again. They needed new designs. They finally decided to send a delegation to talk to Cotterpin.

Meanwhile Cotterpin sat at her drawing board, looking sadly at her nice sharp pencils and her nice blank paper. "Not much point in doing anything," she said to herself. "The Perfect Building is already done."

But she couldn't stop herself. She reached for a pencil and began doodling. "Hmmm," she murmured. "A spiral spire. Nice idea—very, very nice." She doodled some more. "Hey!" she said to herself. "This is really fun!"

At that moment, there was a knock at the door. It was the workers' delegation.

"Cotterpin," began Drillbit, "it's not that we don't love your design, but we're—"

"Bored!" said Cotterpin. "We're all bored. What we really love to do is work!"

"Why don't we just let the Fraggles eat the new building and then get to work again?" suggested Crankshaft. The whole delegation cheered.

Cotterpin was already drawing a big sign. It had a large red arrow on it. THIS WAY TO ECHO CAVERN, it read. ALL YOU CAN EAT!

The next morning, Cotterpin was hard at work when the Architect walked in, looking fit as a fiddle.

"Good morning," he said. "I just passed by your new building. Or what's left of it, anyway. Looks like it was nice work."

"Nice?" Cotterpin grinned. "It was perfect! But wait till you see the one I'm working on now. It's going to be even better!"